Little Joe Chickapig

By Brian Calhoun

Illustrations by Pat Bradley and Brian Calhoun

Thanks to:
Ann Kingston for making me write this book.

The Chickapig team: Mark Rebein, Dave Matthews, Fenton Williams,
and everyone else who has helped bring Chickapig to life.

Studio Fun International
An imprint of Printers Row Publishing Group
A division of Readerlink Distribution Services, LLC
10350 Barnes Canyon Road, Suite 100, San Diego, CA 92121
www.studiofun.com

Copyright © 2018 Chickapig LLC. All rights reserved.

Written by Brian Calhoun
Illustrated by Pat Bradley and Brian Calhoun

Printers Row Publishing Group is a division of Readerlink Distribution Services, LLC.
Studio Fun International is a registered trademark of Readerlink Distribution Services, LLC.

All notations of errors or omissions should be addressed to Studio Fun International,
Editorial Department, at the above address.

ISBN: 978-0-7944-4452-5
Manufactured, printed, and assembled in Stevens Point, Wisconsin, U.S.A.
Third printing, May 2019. WOR/05/19
23 22 21 20 19   3 4 5 6 7

chick·a·pig

/ˈchi-kə-pig/
noun: chickapig; plural noun: chickapigs

1. An animal hybrid that is half-chicken and half-pig.

Little Joe Chickapig lived on a farm,
A farm full of chickapigs and chickapig charm.
For Little Joe Chickapig, still just a boy,
The farm full of chickapigs brought him no joy.

He dreamed of new places beyond the fields,
Sailing vast oceans with swords and with shields.
He hoped he'd find courage to follow his heart.
But how could he do it? How could he start?

The chickapig farm was all that he knew,
With its crops and fields, and cows that poo'd,
And birds, and bees, and horses and goats.
Why was he dreaming of castles and moats?

Joe had an old grandpa, brave and bold,
A chickapig hero who broke the mold.
Joe had an old grandpa, a sailor of seas.
A chickapig hero who lived so free.

"But how? How? How did he go?
How did he do it? How did he know
To follow his heart against the tide?
How did he do it?"
the young Chickapig cried.

"I'll tell you a tale," his mother said.
"I'll tell a tale, before I put you to bed.
Grandpa back then, he was scared too.
Grandpa back then, did not know what to do.

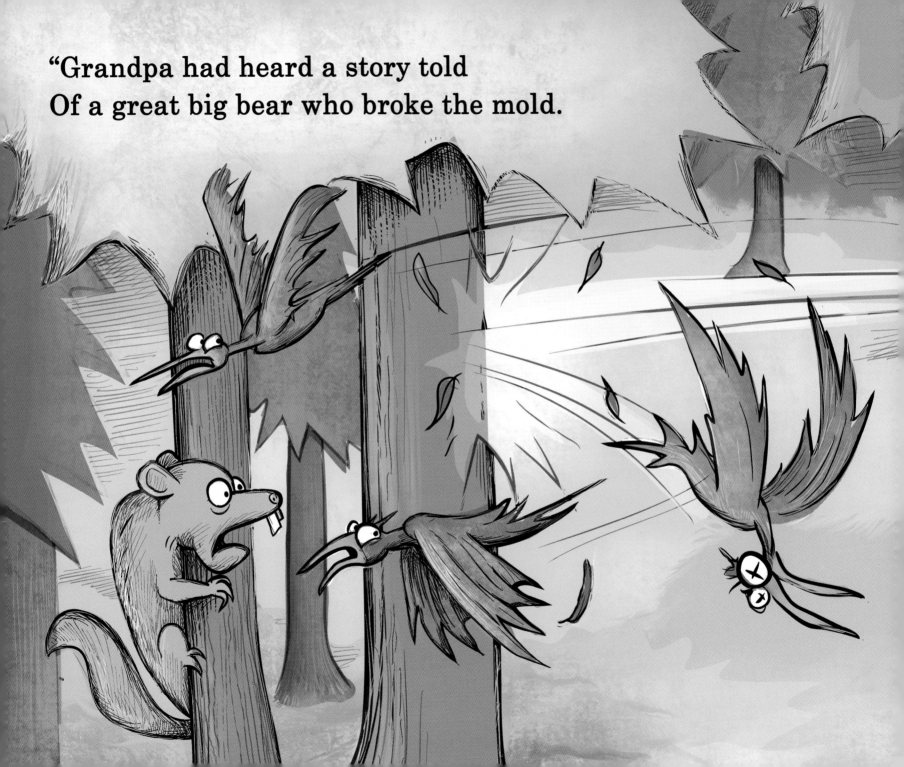

"Grandpa had heard a story told
Of a great big bear who broke the mold.

The bear was tired of striking fear
In all who saw him, all who came near.
The bear had learned quite a skill:
To heal the sick and those struck ill.

"A doctor he became, my son,
To heal the wounds of everyone.
And those who used to run away
Now stood before him every day.

"The bear saw patients one by one.
Never again would anyone run.
The bear became a friend, you see,
To every creature beneath the trees."

"But how? How? How did he go?
How did he do it? How did he know
To follow his heart against the tide?
How did he do it?"
the young Chickapig cried.

"The bear found courage from the strangest place:
He'd heard of a mouse who went to space.

"The mouse, she traveled to the moon and Mars.
The mouse, she traveled amongst the stars.
Her ship, it soared from earth to space,
But in that world, she found her place."

"But how? How? How did she go?
How did she do it? How did she know
To follow her heart against the tide?
How did she do it?"
the young chickapig cried.

"The mouse, she'd heard a story told
Of a fierce young dragon, brave and bold.

"The dragon was known across the land.
She gave up her kingdom to join a band.
She sang her songs, she strummed her guitar.
Her music was heard both near and far."

"But how? How? How did she go?
How did she do it? How did she know
To follow her heart against the tide?
How did she do it?"
the young Chickapig cried.

"There was a warrior from that land
Back before the dragon's band.

"He was a chickapig just like you,
Filled with wonder and feeling blue.
Tired of shields and swords to wield,
He lay down his weapons and planted a field.

"The chickapig farm became all that he knew,
With its crops and fields, and cows that poo'd,
And birds, and bees, and horses and goats.
And never a thought of castles or moats!

"Now Joe, my child, I hope you will see:
Follow your dreams, whatever they be.
And one day in the future when you are old,
Your very own story just might be told."